Seasonal Allergies

Katherine DiSavino
and
Kevin Mead

SAMUELFRENCH.COM
SAMUELFRENCH-LONDON.CO.UK

FOR PRODUCTION ENQUIRIES

UNITED STATES AND CANADA
Info@SamuelFrench.com
1-866-598-8449

UNITED KINGDOM AND EUROPE
Plays@SamuelFrench-London.co.uk
020-7255-4302

Each title is subject to availability from Samuel French, depending upon country of performance. Please be aware that *SEASONAL ALLERGIES* may not be licensed by Samuel French in your territory. Professional and amateur producers should contact the nearest Samuel French office or licensing partner to verify availability.

MUSIC USE NOTE

Licensees are solely responsible for obtaining formal written permission from copyright owners to use copyrighted music in the performance of this play and are strongly cautioned to do so. If no such permission is obtained by the licensee, then the licensee must use only original music that the licensee owns and controls. Licensees are solely responsible and liable for all music clearances and shall indemnify the copyright owners of the play(s) and their licensing agent, Samuel French, against any costs, expenses, losses and liabilities arising from the use of music by licensees. Please contact the appropriate music licensing authority in your territory for the rights to any incidental music.

IMPORTANT BILLING AND CREDIT REQUIREMENTS

If you have obtained performance rights to this title, please refer to your licensing agreement for important billing and credit requirements.

SEASONAL ALLERGIES was originally produced at the Rainbow Dinner Theatre in Pennsylvania in the Winter of 2013. The cast was as follows:

JULIA SHELBY . . . . Josey Miller

THOMAS SHELBY . . . . Scott Russell

CHARLIE SHELBY . . . . Chris Roe

PETE DUMBOWSKI . . . . Christopher Babcock

J.D. CUSIMANO . . . . Jimmy Cosentino

ALISON CUSIMANO. . . . . Rachel Blauberg

EMILY CANTWELL. . . . . Lauren Zehr

CHARACTERS

JULIA SHELBY – 39; professional chef and owner of a local restaurant in West Chester, NY

THOMAS SHELBY – 39; Web/Graphic Designer, works from home, developed and sold an extremely popular mobile gaming app

CHARLIE SHELBY – 8-10; loves karate

PETE DUMBOWSKI – 35; a dentist; in the midst of a year-long divorce Julia's younger brother

J.D. CUSIMANO – 40; runs his family's florist shop; loves the New York Jets

ALISON CUSIMANO – 38; a lawyer; 8 months into a rather unexpected pregnancy and despite all her complaining, loving every minute of it

EMILY CANTWELL – 30s; neighbor of Julia and Thomas; widow

SETTING

Thanksgiving, Christmas and New Year's in Julia and Thomas Shelby's Westchester County home. It's an open first floor, with a living room, kitchen and dining room all coexisting in a fluid layout.

CASTING NOTE

CHARLIE SHELBY can be played by a boy or a girl. For a boy, the full name is Charles Shelby. For a girl, the full name is Charlotte Shelby.

ACT ONE

Scene One

*(Lights up on **JULIA** and **THOMAS SHELBY**'s Westchester County home. It's an open first floor, with a sunken living room (Down Stage Left), Kitchen (Upstage Left) and Dining Room (Down Stage Right) all coexisting in a fluid layout. Stairs (or a hallway to unseen stairs) that lead to the second floor of the house are tucked into the Upstage Right corner of the home. A large bay window is angled near the dining room table, the small hedges growing outside the pane visible to the audience.)*

(This home is perfect for a family.)

*(It's Thanksgiving and preparations for the massive feast that is about to take place are still being made. **ALISON CUSIMANO** (38 years old and 8 months pregnant with a baby that was a bit of surprise) and **JULIA SHELBY** are in the kitchen. **JULIA** has the oven door open and is basting the turkey. She's a professional chef and moves confidently in her domain. **ALISON**, a lawyer, is a bit uncomfortable in this realm, a bit uncomfortable being told what to do, and a bit uncomfortable with a child kicking inside her. But she's very hungry, so she's helping to hurry this process along.)*

*(**THOMAS SHELBY** and **JEAN-DOMENICO (JD) CUSIMANO** sit on the couch, watching football. They are Jets fans, and as such, are seasonally depressed.)*

THOMAS. It's Thanksgiving for crying out loud. Arguably, the most American of all holidays. You think that the New York Jets would have the patriotism to at least kick a field goal by halftime.

JD. I need another beer.

JULIA. From the way the game is going, it sounds like you need ten more beers.

ALISON. God, I want a beer.

JULIA. How about another sparkling grape juice?

ALISON. I'm 38 and pregnant with my first kid. I need a shot of vodka, a turkey leg, and a nap. But I guess I'll take a grape juice. On the rocks. With a twist.

JULIA. That's the spirit.

(**ALISON** *hunts for a task in the kitchen.*)

THOMAS/JD. AH! Come ON! You gotta be kidding me.

(**JULIA** *catches* **ALISON** *sprinkling garlic powder on the string beans, slaps her hand with a spatula. Hands her a flute of grape juice.*)

JULIA. Listen, pregnant lady – you're in my kitchen. I wouldn't waddle into the courtroom and start reciting rulings while you were working.

ALISON. I'm just adding a little zest!

JULIA. Back away from the Garlic Powder and open this can of cranberry sauce.

ALISON. What, the professional chef isn't making us homemade cranberry sauce?

JULIA. The professional chef's husband has the same taste-palate as our eight year old.

THOMAS. I want my cranberry sauce to look like the can it came in. Just as the good Lord intended.

JD. It's Thanksgiving. If it's not brown, I'm not eating it.

ALISON. Is that how you'll teach our child to eat? JD hasn't touched a vegetable in 15 years.

JD. I had the steak salad at Julia's restaurant last week.

ALISON. Yeah, and you ate the steak and left the salad for me.

JD. Well, salad sucks.

THOMAS. A FUMBLE? A FUMBLE? I can't watch this anymore.

(**CHARLIE SHELBY** *(8–10, can be played by a boy or girl)*, *runs across the living room dressed in a Karate outfit.*)

(*He Karate chops at invisible foes.*)

(*No one pays much attention. This is normal. The boys continue to watch the game.* **ALISON** *slices a block of cheese with a knife.*)

CHARLIE. *(OS)* HIYA! HIYA! HIIIIIYA!

JULIA. *(to* **CHARLIE***)* Dinner's almost ready.

CHARLIE. Okay! I just have fifty ninjas left to fight. Can I have that knife?

ALISON. No.

CHARLIE. Okay!

(**CHARLIE** *exits.*)

(**ALISON** *straightens the place settings, waddling her way around the dining room table.*)

JULIA. Alison, stop fidgeting. Can you just sit down for two minutes?

ALISON. I need something to do! Isn't Thanksgiving about everybody bringing something to the table?

JD. Babe, if you'll remember, we were going to bring something to the table. But you burnt it.

ALISON. I've represented enough criminals to know some pretty choice spots to dump your body and get away with it.

JD. Love you too, babe.

JULIA. Hey! The potatoes are almost ready – Alison, do you want to do the honors and mash?

ALISON. Can I eat cheese at the same time?

JULIA. *(wants to say "No.")* Of course. Okay, now let's see what we've got here.

(*She picks up her chef notebook from the counter and opens to her menu list page*)

Turkey's almost done, packed full of stuffing – oyster in the neck, sausage in the butt –

(**CHARLIE** *runs back through the living room.*)

CHARLIE. You said butt!

THOMAS. Your mother is allowed to say butt when she's talking about dinner!

JULIA. – cranberry sauce is out in all of its gelatinous glory –

THOMAS. *(re: Cranberries)* WOO!

ALISON. Potatoes are about to be mashed –

JULIA. *(as she opens the oven door)* The green-bean casserole is baked and going in now to get warmed up –

CHARLIE. BOOOO GREEN-BEANS!

JULIA. Sides: Sweet corn, caramelized apples, brussels sprouts, sweet potato pie, zucchini, Spinach, peas – and of course my balsamic roasted carrots and parsnips!
I feel like there's something missing, though. Shoot, did I forget something?

(There is a beat. Everyone thinks. After a moment:)

JD/THOMAS/ALISON. Pearl onions.

CHARLIE. Ugh, gross.

*(**CHARLIE** runs offstage.)*

ALISON. The smell…

THOMAS. The smell? The taste…

JULIA. Technically pearl onions act as a balancer. It's a strong but very simple taste that you can use to –

THOMAS. None of us believe you.

JULIA. Pete always liked them. They've been his favorite since we were kids. I'm gonna make them.

THOMAS. Well, Pete's not coming. Who else here is going to eat pearl onions – show of hands.

(No one raises their hand.)

JULIA. Pete has a lot on his mind now with the divorce, okay? He could still show up.

THOMAS. Twelve year's we've been doing Friendsgiving. Twelve years. And has a single one of us ever cancelled?

JD. No!

THOMAS. That's right! Not even the year that Alison got Hepatitis B from that sketchy pizza place and we made her eat in the mud room.

ALISON. We agreed never to speak of that.

THOMAS. The point is: we honor tradition. No matter what. For years. Until now…

JULIA. Sweetie, could you get off the soap box and help me carve the bird?

THOMAS. I can carve just fine from up here.

ALISON. Look at the bright side. We never have to have Thanksgiving with Margaret again.

JD. I'll drink to that. Pinkies up in remembrance of Margaret.

(**ALISON, JD,** *and* **THOMAS** *raise their glasses with their pinkies extended gracefully.*)

JULIA. However we all felt about Margaret doesn't change the fact that Pete loved her –

THOMAS. Did he though? And that doesn't *change the fact* that once they got married Pete ghosted on our friendship…

JULIA. What…what does that even mean?

THOMAS. Ghosting. When you leave a party without saying goodbye to anybody. You disappear. Like a ghost does! The point is: Bros before hoes.

JD. YES!

ALISON.	**JULIA.**
Excuse me?	Are you freakin' serious?

THOMAS. No – no. In this scenario we –

(he gestures to all of them)

All of us – including Pete – are the bros. The hoe is Margaret!

JULIA. You're the hoe.

ALISON/JD. *(like "oh snap!")* Oooooh!

JULIA. Pete is your friend and your brother-in-law and you're trash talking him behind his back.

THOMAS. I'd say all this to his face!

JULIA. Would you? Honestly?

(**THOMAS** *subsides.*)

I'm just as disappointed as you all are that Pete cancelled on us, okay? But he's working through some stuff and he needs us – and our good thoughts. Okay?

(**JD** *raises his glass.*)

JD. Let's have a toast to Pete!

(*Everyone raises their glasses.*)

JULIA. To Pete – may true love and happiness be in his future.

THOMAS. May he find his way back to his true friends, who will be here for him, no matter what.

(**JULIA** *smiles at* **THOMAS**. *He squeezes her hand.*)

JD. And may he make it out of the divorce will his balls intact.

ALISON. Hear, hear!

(*They clink glasses and drink.*)

JULIA. You know, I bought the pearl onions, maybe I should just make them – in his honor.

JD/TOM/ALISON/CHARLIE. *(OS)* NO.

(**JULIA** *relents. She dumps the potatoes from a pot into a colander in the sink. Once the water has been strained, she returns the potatoes to the pot and puts it on the counter in front of* **ALISON**.*)

ALISON. Mixer.

(**JULIA** *hands her the mixer.*)

JULIA. Check.

ALISON. Butter.

JULIA. Here you are.

ALISON. Milk.

JULIA. There you go.

ALISON. Salt, pepper, garlic powder.

JULIA. You need to cool it with that garlic powder, lady. You're gonna induce labor.

ALISON. Who is in charge of mashing these potatoes Julia?

JULIA. You are?

ALISON. Damn right. Step aside, chef.

(Sounds from the TV:)

TV ANNOUNCER. …12 seconds left in the half, 4th and 2… They've got 4 receivers on the line. Shotgun. There's the snap. And…it's a bomb. Down the field for Jennings. Up the sideline, one on one, at the 20, and…intercepted by Blackburn!

JD & THOMAS. Nooooo.

JD.   **THOMAS.**

Mother Fuc-   SON OF A –

*(**ALISON** turns the mixer on and drowns out **JD** and **THOMAS**' obscenities. **CHARLIE** enters.)*

CHARLIE. Awwwwwwwwwwwww. Daddy and JD swore!

*(**CHARLIE** chops them with the plastic sword. **THOMAS** picks him up and puts him between them on the couch.)*

JULIA. Charles, do not hit people with your sword.

CHARLIE. It's a Katana.

JD. Hey! You think I'm just a florist don't you? Well it's a cover. I'm really a CIA agent. And I'm on a mission to take you out, Charles Shelby, Karate Master.

*(**JD** gives **CHARLIE** a noogie.)*

CHARLIE. I'm a sensei – and I'm hungry! Did you make something this year Aunt Alison?

ALISON. No.

CHARLIE. Good.

ALISON. Hey!

JULIA. Alright, sensei, go ahead and put the silverware out.

CHARLIE. *(bows to **JULIA**)* Okie-dokie, Mommy-san.

*(**CHARLIE** begins setting the table.)*

*(**ALISON** and **JULIA** maneuver the massive turkey out of the oven. **ALISON** keeps trying to pick at it, **JULIA** keeps swatting her away.)*

JULIA. *(holds up the carving knife)* Boys, will you do the honors?

THOMAS. You got it, mommy-san.

*(***ALISON*** transfers the mashed potatoes to a bowl and brings it over to the table.)*

*(The boys approach the bird and begin to carve away while **JULIA** starts transporting the many sides to the table. The boys and **ALISON** pick at the turkey when **JULIA** isn't looking.)*

JULIA. *(threatening with a ladle)* Hey! Children. Bring that over here and sit.

THOMAS. Yes ma'am.

JULIA. Charlie, you want sparkling grape juice like Aunt Alison?

ALISON. You and me kid, we're the sober senseis.

*(***THOMAS*** transfers the turkey carvings to a plate and carries it over to the table. He probably is singing the theme song to the Olympics.)*

THOMAS. Let the 12th annual Thanksgiving games begin!

JD. C'mon Chuck! Sit by me!

*(***JD*** pulls a chair out for **CHARLIE**. Everyone takes their seat around the table.)*

THOMAS. Our first event will now commence: The Feast.

ALISON. Finally. I've been training for eight months.

THOMAS. Followed by our second event: Naps.

JD/ALISON.	**CHARLIE.**
Naps!	BOO!

THOMAS. And lastly, the third and final event, in which I happen to be 11 year reigning champion of the world: Leftover Sandwiches.

JULIA. Before the games begin, we must first hold the opening ceremonies.

ALISON. They better be QUICK opening ceremonies. This baby is hungry, Julia.

JULIA. Thanksgiving has always been my favorite holiday – and not just because I love cooking and it's a day all about the food. I love it because it gives me a chance to be with my family and friends. To talk, and eat, and nap –

EVERYONE. *(Raising their glasses)* NAPS!

JULIA. Because a lot of things change over the years – everything… Jobs, and houses, and new additions *(to* **ALISON***)*, but friends are the constant. Friends that are family. I'm thankful that wherever we are and whatever we're going through, that we'll have each other no matter what. I love our crazy family.

THOMAS. To family.

ALL. To family.

JD. And to divorce –

ALISON. *(Kicking* **JD***)* Shh!

JD. Only when absolutely necessary.

(CRASH. The sound of a car hitting a tree somewhere down the block.)

(They glance at each other. Did that sound like – no, everything is fine.)

JULIA. Let's all go around the table and say what we're thankful for. Like I said, I'm thankful for all you knuckleheads.

ALISON. I'll go next. I'm thankful I've got a bun in the oven and a table of food in front of me. And I'll be even more thankful when you guys say your piece quickly so we can dig in.
(Threateningly)
Got it?

JD. *(Quickly jumping in)* I'm thankful for Alison! And my floral shop – business is a'blooming! Get it?

ALISON. Yes, we get it. Very good.

*(**PETE** now appears in the kitchen window. He has bush branches in his hair and clothes.)*

THOMAS. I'm thankful there's always a "next season" for the Jets.

(**THOMAS** *and* **JD** *high five*)

And that Charlie is taking karate so he can protect us from all those ninjas!

(**THOMAS** *and* **CHARLIE** *high five*)

CHARLIE. I'm thankful for my karate teacher and for Aunt Alison's baby, cause it means I can finally sit at a kids table with someone!

ALISON. Great! Let's dig in.

(ANOTHER CRASH. This time, tin garbage cans – and it sounds like it came from the front yard.)

(Everyone reacts, goes to the window except for **ALISON**, *who begins serving herself and starts to eat.)*

THOMAS. Well. Better late than never, I guess.

ALISON. Describe what's happening. I'm starving –

JULIA. Pete!

(The front door opens. **PETE DUMBOWSKI** *enters, carrying four pie boxes from the A&P. He is a dentist in his mid-30s, currently disheveled – but by circumstance, not by nature.)*

(Everyone but **THOMAS** *gives a cheer when* **PETE** *walks in.)*

PETE. Sorry I'm late!

THOMAS. Late? …you cancelled on us this morning.

PETE. *(Totally knows what he's talking about)* I have no idea what you're talking about.

JULIA. It doesn't matter. I told you he would come!

*(***JULIA*** puts a protective arm around* **PETE** *and ushers him into the room – she shoots* **THOMAS** *a dirty look as she passes.)*

Charlie, grab another place setting for Uncle Pete.

*(***CHARLIE*** sets another place at the table.)*

JD. So – ah – what happened out there man? You okay? Your car looks a little banged up.

PETE. Yeah it is, isn't it? I blew a tire and hit a Douglas Fir.

(to **CHARLIE***)*

That's a type of Christmas tree.

(to all)

Since I was so close to getting here I just decided to keep going. But then I hit your trash cans because I couldn't steer the car. But everything is fine. Except for the front end of my car, both axles, and the tree. And your trash cans. You should get new trash cans. We can run to Home Depot later.

JD. Uh – Pete, should we call a tow company or something?

ALISON. Or a doctor?

PETE. Oh, no. It's fine. I mean –

(he looks to his sister)

As long as it's okay with Thomas and Julia if I leave the car in their driveway? Just for…a little?

| **THOMAS.** | **JULIA.** |
| No. | Of course! |

THOMAS. I'm just having a little trouble here Pete. I don't understand how you can break twelve years of tradition with ONE phone call and then just show up and pretend like the betrayal never happened.

ALISON. "Betrayal" seems a little extreme.

THOMAS. Let's call it what it is!

PETE. *(as he hands the pie boxes to* **JULIA***)* You know what? I have found recently that my life has been a bit inconsistent. So I'm just learning to embrace it! Like today for instance: I woke up and I knew I wanted to eat a pie – this morning it was cherry, but then I wanted banana cream and at the A&P I couldn't stop thinking about pumpkin. So instead of deciding on one I got four. Just in case. Cuz you know, who knows these days what might happen from one moment to the next. One second you're married, in a committed, life-long relationship – and the next you're not in a committed, life-long relationship, and you have nothing of value to depend on. The world is completely unpredictable!

ALISON. Preach.

JULIA. *(uncertain)* Thanks, Pete. This is great.

*(**JULIA** takes the pies into the kitchen as everyone retakes their seats at the dining room table.)*

THOMAS. *(mutters)* You sound like a crazy person.

JULIA. Thomas, remember how sad we were when we thought Pete wasn't coming – and how disappointed you felt? But now he's here. Pete, my brother, and your best friend, is here now. So let's lock it up, Shelby, and be happy. Okay?

*(Everyone begins serving themselves food. **ALISON** takes seconds.)*

PETE. "Be Happy!" What a great motto! I'm going to put it down on my list of potential new mottos!

*(**PETE** goes to take out a notebook from his pocket, but it's not there.)*

Ugh. I must have left my life journal at the Inn.

ALISON. The Inn?

PETE. Yes, the Red Roof Inn.

JULIA. Why are you staying at the Red Roof Inn?

PETE. Because I gave my house to Margaret.

ALL. WHAT?

ALISON. Pete, why would you do that? You bought that house years before you and Margaret got married…please tell me you didn't sign anything over to her.

PETE. No. But I did help her change all the locks.

JULIA. Pete, you love that house.

PETE. Yes. Yes I do.

CHARLIE. Uncle Pete. are you sad? You're talking loud and happy, but you seem real sad. You want some of my sparkling grape juice?

PETE. Yes. And yes.

THOMAS. No. Someone pour this man a real drink.

(**PETE** *smiles at* **THOMAS,** *thankful.*)

PETE. I would like both a grape juice and a real drink.

JULIA. On it.

(**JULIA** *gets up to make his drink and pour the grape juice.*)

PETE. I wonder what Margaret is doing in my house right now. Do you guys think she's enjoying her dinner?

ALISON. Peter. Look at me. You are under no legal obligations to give Margaret your house. Why did you do that?

PETE. She wanted it.

ALISON. Well, I want to be a size 4 again, but that ain't happening.

JD. Ali, we don't know what's been going on. Margaret might get the house no matter what Pete wants.

ALISON. Well, that doesn't mean he has to just lay down and not fight for it. Pete didn't want the divorce. Margaret did.

PETE. I appreciate your concern, Alison, but Margaret can be very persuasive. And you know me –

JD.	**ALISON.**
You're a pushover?	You can't say no.

THOMAS.	**JULIA.**
You never think things through?	You're very sensitive.

PETE. What? No. I was gonna say I'm generous to the people I care about.

ALISON. Pete. You are the only one of my friends with a swimming pool. I want my kid to swim in your swimming pool.

PETE. I do miss my swimming pool.

JULIA. I think what Ali is trying to say is that we're just worried about you. That you're letting Margaret take too much.

ALISON. Like my swimming pool.

THOMAS. Look – material things aside. You've let this woman trample on your life enough already. And if we're being honest, Peter, you're my brother-in-law and my best friend and I say this with all due respect, but when you married that woman, you were out of your mind.

PETE. I appreciate your support in my time of need, Tom. What a nice thing to say to your *best friend.* You know what, if you guys all think I'm some big pushover, then I'll just leave.

(**PETE** *stands up.*)

ALL. Sit down.

(**PETE** *sits down.*)

THOMAS. I'm sorry. I'm not trying to be mean. I'm just saying you had a lot going for you before Margaret even came into your life –

PETE. Like what?

JULIA. Your friends, your family, your dental practice.

THOMAS. You love what you do, and you're great at it. That's a rare thing, not everyone can say that…

PETE. I – ah. I actually closed down the practice.

JULIA. Pete. Are you kidding me?

PETE. …temporarily. Sort of. I just needed a break from everything.

(*The friends exchange a look. This is not normal.*)

JULIA. (*processing*) Okay – that's okay.

(*Everyone looks at* **JULIA.**)

THOMAS. (*to* **PETE**) No. It's not. You changed everything for this person. I want the real Pete back. Don't you?

PETE. I don't know.

JULIA. No. Pete. It's fine. I understand. This has been a really tough time for you, and you just need to collect your thoughts –

PETE. Right! Exactly.

JULIA. You know, you should look at this an opportunity to hit the reset button. You have the chance to do whatever you want. Take a vacation. Get a new car. Clean some teeth.

THOMAS. But not because of Margaret.

JD. Yeah. It's all about what you want, now, dude. You're not tied down anymore! No wife, no kids…you're free!

ALISON. *(to JD)* Excuse me?

(JD stuffs food into his mouth.)

PETE. You're right. And what I want…is pearl onions.

JULIA. Then you shall have pearl onions, little brother.

THOMAS. …I guess that's a start.

(JULIA goes to the kitchen and starts making the pearl onions. The others groan.)

JULIA. *(to them)* Can it.

(to PETE)

See? If you need something, we've got you covered. We're your family.

JD. That's what we're here for, Petey.

ALISON. Clearly, you need us.

PETE. Thanks guys. I just don't want to be a burden.

THOMAS. Don't be ridiculous.

JULIA. You know what?… You should stay with us.

THOMAS. What?

CHARLIE. Yeah!

PETE. Really?

JULIA. Yes, of course! Pete, stay with us.

ALISON. And while you're staying here, I can help you figure out how to get your house back.

THOMAS. Now hang on –

PETE. – Oh, gosh. I don't know. Margaret doesn't like it when you take things away from her.

ALISON. Pete, do you want your house back?

PETE. Yes. I think I really do.

ALISON. Then let me be your legal counsel on this, and we'll get it back for you. And I'll be real nice to Margaret and her lawyers about it. How does that sound?

JULIA. See, Pete? This is perfect! You can stay with us for a couple days while Alison and you figure out your house situation. Right Charlie? Right Thomas?

CHARLIE. YEAH! You can sleep in my bunk bed! You get the bottom bunk.

PETE. That's good. Because I'm afraid of heights.

JULIA. Uncle Pete can have his own room, Charlie. The living room!

PETE. This is amazing, you guys! Thank you. I'll just go grab my suitcase. I left it in the car.

(PETE *exits*)

THOMAS. You need help with the pearl onions?

JULIA. No, I'm good.

THOMAS. I'm going to help you with the pearl onions.

(**THOMAS** *corners* **JULIA** *in the kitchen.* **JD**, **ALISON** *and* **CHARLIE** *continue to feast.*)

He had his stuff with him, Julia. He knew you would feel bad for him and tell him to stay with us.

JULIA. He needs to be with his family –

THOMAS. You're enabling him! The man needs to work through this on his own. Otherwise he's never gonna come out of it. And what about the horror stories you used to tell me about when you were kids?

JULIA. First of all, he was messy when he was twelve, okay? He's a grown man, now. I think we can trust him to take care of himself. And second of all, what about all that talk about loyalty and friendship? Your best friend needs you. This is your chance to be there for him. Besides – it's just going to be for a couple of days!

THOMAS. But what if it takes longer than that?

JULIA. Watch. A couple days here with us and Pete will be a new man.

(**PETE** *re-enters, holding a HUGE black trash bag [it is filled with dirty laundry] and dragging a rolling suitcase with him.*)

PETE. This is going to be really great, you guys. Just like the old days, right Jules? Except I have an earlier bed time now.

JD. What's in the bag, Pete?

PETE. This? This is just all of my dirty clothes.

(*The garbage bag breaks, piles of dirty laundry explode from the bottom.*)

Darnit!

THOMAS. Here, let me help you –

PETE. Nah, it's okay. Just leave them. I'll clean it up tomorrow Oh man! Julia! Those pearl onions smell AMAZING. Just like mom used to make!

(**PETE** *leaves his rolling suitcase and spilled clothes in the middle of the living room floor. He sits down at the table and picks up his fork and knife.*)

I'm ready!

(**THOMAS** *shoots a look at* **JULIA** *as she plates the pearl onions and brings them over to the table. She puts them in front of* **PETE.**)

JULIA. Okay. Here we go.

PETE. Oh boy! You guys! Wait! I just had a great idea. Don't worry about the Christmas tree. I know the PERFECT one for us to have for the holidays. Some of the lower branches are missing, but the top of it is perfect. It's a Douglas Fir!

(*Everyone exchanges a glance.* **PETE** *digs into the pearl onions.*)

I love Thanksgiving.

(*blackout*)

Scene Two

(Lights up. The day after Thanksgiving.)

(It is very, very early in the morning. Like, maybe 5:30 AM. Epic classical music, in the style of the Game of Thrones *theme song, plays from the boom-box in the kitchen.*)*

(The living room is even more of a disaster. Makeshift bedding and **PETE***'s belongings look like they've exploded all over the place.* **PETE** *is nowhere in sight.)*

*(***THOMAS***, however, is. And so is the Thanksgiving turkey, half-covered in tinfoil on the kitchen counter.)*

(Next to the carcass, **THOMAS** *puts the finishing cranberry sauce and corn touches on a HUGE leftovers sandwich, dancing and spreading mustard in time with the epic sound track playing behind him – this is the kind of sandwich dreams are made of. It's 5:30 AM, and* **THOMAS** *is the happiest man in the world.)*

(He conducts the orchestra and prepares the sandwich for the first glorious bite. **JULIA** *comes down the stairs. She's dressed and ready to go.)*

JULIA. *(RE: The sandwich)* Starting a little early?

THOMAS. This day is starting a little early.

JULIA. We have to get there before the crowds.

THOMAS. *(conducting, about to take a bite)* Shh. This is the best part. BUM badadadadum, DADADADADUM-daaa DUM

JULIA. *(seeing the living room for the first time)* OH MY GOD!

*(***THOMAS** *jumps at the sound of her voice – startled before he could chomp into the sandwich.)*

THOMAS. What?

---

* The publisher recommends that the licensee creates an original composition that stays true to the authors' intent.

JULIA. Look at this mess!

(she glances around, whispers)

Where is he? He said he was going to clean this up!

THOMAS. Uh. I don't know. He wasn't here when I came down. Ba-dum, badada, DUM, BA DA DUM. Ugh. I love this music. It's preparing us for battle – me vs. this sandwich, you vs. the other crazies on Black Friday.

(more singing –)

BA-DUM, BADADA, DUM –

JULIA. *(trying to get him to stop)* Tom? TOM. Please.

THOMAS. You're the one that insisted he stay here, Jules. Technically this is your mess.

JULIA. We have so much to do today and I – I just –

THOMAS. Relax. Make a sandwich. Have some coffee. Take a Xanax.

JULIA. Can you please ask Pete and Charlie to tidy this up before we come home?

THOMAS. He's your brother. You're the one who invited him to stay. You ask him to –

(stops mid-bite again)

Hang on. Pete and Charlie don't have to come Black Friday shopping with us?

JULIA. No?

THOMAS. *(drops his sandwich)* That's not fair, dude!

JULIA. Tough ta-tas, dude. You're my husband and I need you to defend my honor against the other crazies in the store.

THOMAS. Why can't all the boys stay home together? There's an army of leftovers and it's my sworn duty to eat them.

JULIA. Thomas. We are shopping for our son.

(Game of Thrones reference...)

Christmas is coming.

THOMAS. It's really sexy when you make Game of Thrones references with me.

(**JULIA** *picks up his sandwich and takes a huge bite.*)

Hey! Not sexy! Extremely rude.

JULIA. *(mouth full)* This is so good!

THOMAS. I KNOW! Give it!

JULIA. Hold on – I just need to –

(She takes another HUGE bite.)

(**THOMAS** *snatches the sandwich out of* **JULIA***'s hands.*)

THOMAS. You are playing dirty, woman. You are officially ready for Black Friday at the mall.

(The front door opens. **CHARLIE** *and* **PETE** *walk in from outside, both wearing big bulky jackets and carrying a few bags each.)*

Whoa! You guys are up early. Where did you go?

CHARLIE. Uncle Pete wanted us to get –

PETE. *(covering)* Some bags! From my car!

(he holds up the bags he's carrying)

See? Here they are!

(When **JULIA** *and* **THOMAS** *aren't looking,* **PETE** *gives* **CHARLIE** *a shove and gestures for him to keep quiet.)*

JULIA. Tom, we should head out – it's getting late.

PETE. It's 5:45, Jules.

THOMAS. No, Peter. On Black Friday, time no longer exists in a normal continuum. And sandwiches that other people make are recklessly consumed by greedy spouses.

JULIA. Tom, could you also mention the –

(she tries to casually gesture to the mess in the living room)

THOMAS. Oh, right. Pete, Julia had something she wanted to ask you –

(**JULIA** *glares at Tom.*)

JULIA. I want to get the Christmas tree up tonight, so can you just clean up – well, everything. It's a mess in here.

CHARLIE. But Uncle Pete and me are gonna decorate the tree!

JULIA. Oh. Really. That is so. Thoughtful. You know what, we can just all do it together when we're back, OK? Some music, some eggnog, a bottle of scotch for me.

THOMAS. It'll be great. Family tradition!

PETE. It's really no trouble at all, Julia. I love decorating trees! Remember how Mom always had me decorate our tree?

JULIA. That's because Mom hated getting the ornaments down from the attic and –

PETE. Well, I never minded. I loved it!

JULIA. Yeah. And you would do it at 4am when everyone else was asleep so YOU would get all the credit for decorating the tree yourself and nobody ELSE who lived in the house and who ALSO loved Christmas had a chance to help you.

PETE. Like I said – I love decorating trees.

THOMAS. Well, you see, it's OUR family TRADITION to decorate OUR tree together.

JULIA. Why don't you guys wait until we're back and we can do this together – okay?

(**CHARLIE** *has gone over to the kitchen counter and is taking a HUGE bite of the leftover sandwich.*)

THOMAS. Hey! Get away from that. Little scavenger

CHARLIE. s'good, Dad!

THOMAS. THANK YOU.

JULIA. We should go. The tree is in the closet. You guys can clean up here, then take it out and get it ready. How's that sound?

(**THOMAS** *grabs the very small piece of his sandwich that is left and holds it protectively as he backs towards the door.* **JULIA** *follows.*)

THOMAS. Don't eat all the leftovers. I am extremely serious.

(*He exits.*)

JULIA. And don't decorate the tree, okay? Just – take it out of the closet and set it up. After you clean. Clean and then set up the –

CHARLIE. Mom. We got it.

JULIA. Ok. Bye.

(She exits.)

*(***CHARLIE*** *and* ***PETE*** *look at each other. The sound of a car starting and driving off.)*

PETE. Tree in the closet?

CHARLIE. Mom likes the fake ones. No needles to clean up. Also, the real ones make her sneeze.

PETE. Charles. If there's one thing your Uncle Pete will teach you, it is this: If you don't have a real tree it's not real Christmas. It's fake Christmas. You don't just pull Christmas out of the closet and assemble it in pieces. You go out and chop it down with your bare hands. Or your car.

CHARLIE. Can we bring it in now?

PETE. Yes we can.

(They run to the door, open it and disappear outside.)

(A beat.)

(They re-enter, each of them grabbing the side of a haggard evergreen, unevenly covered in needles, and clearly chopped down in a hurry. A victim of ***PETE****'s driving put out of its misery.)*

As soon as I hit this tree with my car last night I knew it was the one. And hiding it in the bushes? A stroke of genius, Charles.

CHARLIE. Thank you!

PETE. Everything comes together in the end. It's all part of a plan bigger than either one of us.

CHARLIE. Is that true, Uncle Pete?

PETE. I have no idea. But it's one of my potential new mottos that I wrote down and it feels good saying it. Let's just – let's set it down over here. We need a stand.

CHARLIE. I think there's one in the closet –

(**CHARLIE** *pulls open the closet door and begins pulling items out in order to get to the stand. Scarves, jackets, boots, blankets, tools, etc all come flying out of the closet until he emerges, victorious, with the Christmas tree stand.*)

PETE. Excellent work, kid! Okay, now let's just clear a space for the tree –

(**PETE,** *in the exact same manner as* **CHARLIE** *going through the closet, begins to toss his paraphernalia out of the way – clothes, shoes, books, toiletries, etc go flying.*)

CHARLIE. Mom said we should clean up first before we –

(**PETE** *uses his foot to push his clothes off to the side, in a more contained pile, leaving a big patch on the floor for the tree stand.*)

PETE. Done. Bring me that tree stand.

(**CHARLIE** *brings over the tree stand. Over the following conversation, the two try to set up the Christmas tree. Neither one is very good at this. They should eventually get it set up in a corner of the living room. If it's leaning against a wall at the end, that's just fine.*)

(*Once it's set up, they might try to rotate the tree to hide large holes from view – this won't be possible.*)

CHARLIE. (*Handing him the tree stand*) Why do you cry so much?

PETE. (*as he struggles with the tree*) Huh? I don't cry.

CHARLIE. You cried last night.

PETE. Dinner made me emotional.

CHARLIE. But you cried during dessert, too. And then after we all went to bed. And then again this morning when we got your car out of the tree.

PETE. Have you ever wrecked your car into a tree? It's traumatic! And why were you listening to me cry last night? You should've been sleeping.

CHARLIE. I was trying to, but you were crying too loud. Are you okay?

PETE. NO!

(*A beat.*)

I mean, yes. I'm just – a little sad.

CHARLIE. Oh.

PETE. Things are changing for me. And I wasn't exactly ready for it.

CHARLIE. I understand, Uncle Pete. This year, I had to move into the elementary school building, and I had to learn all the new rooms and hallways and it was real scary and different. But after awhile, it wasn't different any more. It was normal.

PETE. Yeah. That makes sense. I guess I just haven't learned the hallways yet.

CHARLIE. You will, don't worry.

PETE. Hey – so what did you ask Santa for Christmas?

CHARLIE. A black belt.

PETE. That's very fashion forward of you.

CHARLIE. No, Uncle Pete. A black belt.

(*He demonstrates a karate chop, maybe the tree almost falls over*)

Hiya. What did you ask Santa for?

PETE. A new wife. HAHAHAHHAHAHA.

(**CHARLIE** *looks at him. The perfectly lovely, totally confused stare of an eight year old.*)

Yeah. I stopped asking Santa for presents a long time ago.

CHARLIE. Why? Santa is the best.

PETE. Well, Charlie, after a while, you get to a point where the kinds of things you want, Santa can't just bring down the chimney. And as you get older, you'll learn that those are the things you need more than toys and black belts.

CHARLIE. Like wives?

PETE. Yeah. Like wives. And houses with swimming pools. That you bought after years of hard work at a dental practice you started by yourself.

CHARLIE. That stuff doesn't sound fun. All the stuff Santa brings me is fun. Maybe you should ask Santa for something this year. Something he can bring down the chimney. But not a wife.

PETE. Wives can be fun… Just not my wife.

CHARLIE. Yeah. Aunt Margaret is boring.

PETE. Actually, maybe I'll ask for a black belt too. So I can karate chop her lawyer in the face. That would be fun.

CHARLIE. That would be fun! You should have fun more.

PETE. I have fun! I have lots of fun!

(**CHARLIE** *and* **PETE** *are done setting up the tree. It looks awful. They take a step back and admire their handiwork.*)

CHARLIE. Mom is going to love this.

(*KNOCK KNOCK KNOCK.* **PETE** *and* **CHARLIE** *look at the front door.*)

I'll get it!

(**CHARLIE** *flies to the door and throws it open.* **EMILY CANTWELL** *(30's, loves recycling and Pinterest) stands in the frame.*)

Hello! Who are you?

EMILY. Hi! I'm Emily – Is your mom or –

(*she sees* **PETE**)

Oh. Hi. I live down the road and I'm pretty sure you took a Douglas Fir from my front yard.

PETE. Umm – no. That would be crazy.

EMILY. (*She looks into the room*) Oh, yup. There it is. In your living room.

PETE. Madam, it's Christmas season. And, as you know, many Christmas trees look extremely similar, so you could very well be mistaken.

EMILY. Well, MY Douglas Fir looks like someone hit it with a car last night.

CHARLIE. It's cause he DID hit it with a car last night!

EMILY. Also, I watched you and your son chop it down and carry it off my lawn.

PETE. That's not my son.

EMILY. Just like that's not my tree?

CHARLIE. He's not my dad. He's my Uncle. He lives on the couch and cries a lot.

EMILY. Kid, do you need me to call social services or something? Are you okay?

PETE. We're fine. Everything is fine.

CHARLIE. Do you wanna take your tree back?

EMILY. No, not really. Especially after seeing it up close. I just wanted to swing by, and see, you know…what the heck was wrong with you people.

CHARLIE. He's sad. You want some turkey? It was Thanksgiving yesterday.

EMILY. Um –

PETE. You know what? Yes. That is your tree. I apologize for lying. And I apologize for chopping it down with my car. Please, come have some turkey. It's the least we can do after stealing from you.

EMILY. Well, it's a little early for turkey, isn't it? I should probably head back, anyway –

PETE. We've made a terrible first impression and I'm still not entirely certain you aren't going to leave and call the cops.

EMILY. I was considering it.

PETE. *(quietly to* **EMILY***)* Look, please. Just come in and have some turkey. I'm sorry, I shouldn't have taken your tree, but I was just trying to do something nice for my sister. And, I mean, did you SEE the tree after I hit it? Someone was gonna have to chop it down. So really, I was trying to do something nice for you, too. Please don't call the cops.

EMILY. *(laughing)* Ok. Fair enough. I will have some turkey.

*(***EMILY*** enters. ***PETE*** closes the door after her.)*

(CHARLIE runs over to the kitchen and climbs up on the counter to grab plates out for them. He begins making a sandwich for EMILY.)

PETE. *(quietly)* Thank you.

(to CHARLIE)

See, Charlie? You shouldn't steal. And you shouldn't drive while crying. But if you do, all you have to do is own up to it and everything will be a-OK.

EMILY. Crying? Are you OK?

CHARLIE. I told you, he's sad. He needs a new wife. And Santa can't carry a wife down the chimney.

PETE. Umm – okay. So, some parts of our conversation got taken a bit out of context.

EMILY. I'm so sorry. Did your wife pass?

PETE. She passed on me!

(PETE waits for the joke to land. It doesn't. Moves on–)

No. She's alive. And living in my house. Oh god. I can't stop talking. I think I'd be less nervous if you told me you didn't plan on calling the police.

EMILY. No police. I promise. I actually kind of hated that tree. I just wanted to meet the guy who took it.

PETE. Well. That's me. Pete Dumbowski. Tree thief… Trief? HAHAHA. I'm a dentist. And this is Charlie.

CHARLIE. Do you want mustard on your sandwich?

EMILY. Sure. Why not. We'll call this an early lunch. A really, really early lunch.

(CHARLIE passes her a plate with a sandwich on it.)

CHARLIE. Here you go!

EMILY. This looks lovely. Thank you, Charlie.

(She looks at PETE, who nods encouragingly, and takes a bite. It's really good. She's happily surprised.)

This is awesome!

CHARLIE. Thanks. Uncle Pete, you want one?

PETE. Sure, why not!

(**CHARLIE** *sets about making another sandwich.*)

EMILY. I haven't had a leftovers sandwich like this in – gosh. It's been too long. My husband used to make them. And he'd always laugh at me – but my favorite thing to put on them was pearl onions.

PETE. You're kidding.

EMILY. No. I know, it's gross, right? But I love pearl onions.

PETE. I love pearl onions. We HAVE pearl onions. Do you want pearl onions?

(**PETE** *hops up out of his chair and goes to the fridge, retrieving the bowl of pearl onions.*)

EMILY. Oh my gosh. Yes. We used to make them every year but my mom hates them, so now I never get them.

PETE. Your husband doesn't make them for you anymore?

EMILY. Well, he died. So, no. I'm sorry, that was a little… blunt, wasn't it?

PETE. A little.

EMILY. I have this terrible condition. I say whatever pops into my head.

PETE. That's OK. You're just very…honest. And I'm sorry to hear that.

CHARLIE. Me too. How'd he die?

PETE. Charlie! I'm sorry. He suffers from your condition too.

EMILY. No – it's okay. I brought it up.

(*to* **CHARLIE**)

He got very sick. Not your normal kind of sick – not a cold or the flu or something.

CHARLIE. Was it cancer?

EMILY. Uh – yes. They teach you kids some heavy sh – stuff, huh?

CHARLIE. Yeah. I know karate, too. I'm gonna put on my outfit to show you!

(**CHARLIE** *exits up the stairs.*)

(*A beat.*)

EMILY. Pass those onions, will you?

PETE. I'm sorry – he wasn't trying to –

EMILY. No. It's okay. Really. It happened a few years ago, and it honestly helps to talk about it.

PETE. I feel like a real jerk joking about my divorce, now.

EMILY. Hey, that's not an easy thing to go through, either. Heartbreak is heartbreak.

PETE. Yeah, I guess.

EMILY. So why the divorce? Did you crash your car in her bushes or something?

PETE. Nah, that's how we got married.

(This joke surprises **EMILY.** *She laughs.* **PETE** *is surprised she's laughing. He laughs.)*

(KNOCK KNOCK KNOCK. **PETE** *glances at the door.)*

EMILY. Did you steal a scotch pine from the guy next door, too?

PETE. Sorry – hold on just one second.

(He crosses to the door and opens it. **ALISON** *and* **JD** *stand in the doorway.)*

ALISON. I've got a plan for you to get your house back, but first get out of my way.

JD. She has to pee.

ALISON. I have to pee!

*(***ALISON*** pushes past* **PETE** *and waddles across the kitchen towards the downstairs bathroom. As she passes* **EMILY** *–)*

Hello. I'm Alison. Nice to meet you.

*(***ALISON*** slams the bathroom door.)*

JD. So, yeah, hi, I'm JD. That's my wife. And that's my kid that's pressing on her bladder.

EMILY. Emily. I live a few houses down.

JD. Pleasure to meet you. Just stopping by?

EMILY. Well, I came to solve the mystery of the tree in my yard that went missing.

(she gestures to the tree)

JD. Oh. Nice tree. Wait a minute. No it isn't. Lemme guess: someone hit it with their car?

PETE. Mystery solved!

JD. Why did you bring it inside?

PETE. Well, I was trying to cover my tracks. Which didn't quite work. But, also it's a Christmas tree!

EMILY. Obviously.

JD. Julia is allergic to pine.

PETE. Yeah, I know. But she'll get over it. Christmas isn't Christmas without an evergreen.

EMILY. *(helpfully)* Or an allergy attack!

PETE. Exactly. Wait, what?

*(The toilet flushes. The sink runs. **ALISON** comes waddling out of the bathroom.)*

ALISON. Hi, hello. I'm sorry. When you're pregnant, you're ruled by your bladder. And your stomach. Ooh, a sandwich! Who are you?

*(she picks **PETE**'s sandwich up and begins eating it)*

EMILY. Uh – I'm Emily.

ALISON. Like Madonna? No last name?

EMILY. Cantwell. Emily Cantwell. I live down the road. Your friend stole my tree. I'm just visiting. I feel like I'm being interrogated?

JD. She's a lawyer and she's pregnant. The combination seems to have this effect on people. She made three checkout clerks cry today.

ALISON. But I'm done with my shopping! Up top.

*(**ALISON** and **EMILY** high five)*

So. Emily. You're cute. Are you single? Did he tell you he's a divorced man now?

EMILY. We did talk about that. And my dead husband. We're friends.

ALISON. Oh, your husband is dead? Good. I mean, not good, but you know. Pete's sad. He's a great guy, but he's sad and nobody wants to see him like this. And you're cute. And single. Anyway. Pete. I have a plan about your swimming pool.

PETE. You mean my house?

ALISON. Yes, your house that is attached to your swimming pool.

PETE. JD, Alison knows she's not supposed to drink coffee while she's pregnant, right?

JD. It's adrenaline from power shopping.

ALISON. We got up at 2am. We went, we shopped, we conquered.

JD. With coupons!

(*JD takes the sandwich from* **ALISON**, *moves some clothes to sit on the couch, and turns on the TV.*)

Ahh.

ALISON. *(Re:* **EMILY***'s sandwich)* Do you mind?

EMILY. Go for it.

ALISON. *(takes a bite)* What? Pearl onions? What is this crap? …Actually, it's not that bad.

EMILY. Right?

ALISON. Anyway, Pete. Your house. When you changed all the locks for Margaret and basically handed her over my child's summertime activities, did you sign anything?

PETE. Alison, I just want to point out –

ALISON. Peter. I'm offering you free legal counsel. Will you please shut your face and pass me some more pearl onions?

(**PETE** *hands her the bowl of pearl onions.*)

JD. Hey – is there anymore stuffing?

EMILY. Uh – yeah – it's on the counter. You want some?

JD. Yes please!

(**EMILY** *brings him over the stuffing.*)

Looks like they're doing a Back to the Future Marathon.

EMILY. Oh! I love those movies.

(She sits down with **JD** *and they begin eating the stuffing and watching the TV.)*

ALISON. Did you sign anything for Margaret or her lawyers?

PETE. No – I –

ALISON. Okay. Good. Here's the plan. I'm gonna call her lawyer up and tell him we have an offer, okay?

PETE. I was planning on getting a black belt for Christmas and karate chopping him in the face, but I'm willing to compromise.

ALISON. I'm going to pretend I didn't hear you physically threaten her council. Here's the deal. You're going to pay a little bit more in alimony, and get Margaret set up with a new apartment – down payment, all that. In return, she gives you back your swimming pool.

PETE. My house.

ALISON. Right. You know, I really don't remember why I never liked pearl onions. These are great.

(The front door opens. **TOM** *and* **JULIA** *enter.)*

JULIA. Hello… Everyone?

PETE. You're back! That was really fast –

THOMAS. We forgot the coupons.

JD. DUDE – you gotta remember the coupons.

ALISON. Rookie mistake.

THOMAS. Black Friday is supposed to be for eating, not for shopping!

JD. Welcome to the big leagues.

JULIA. *(digging through stuff on the coffee table)* The coupons were on the coffee table…which is now a hamper. Somehow it's messier in here than when we left. How is that possible?

THOMAS. *(noticing the turkey carcass)* AND THE LEFTOVERS ARE PRACTICALLY GONE. It's not even 8am! How is that possible?

JD. *(holding the bowl of stuffing – offering it out)* Your wife is a really, really good cook.

JULIA. *(inspecting the tree)* This is not the tree from the closet –

EMILY. *(standing up)* Um. No. It's from my front yard.

(JULIA sneezes.)

I'm Emily –

THOMAS. Oh – hey! I've seen you around – you live down the block, right?

JULIA. *(sneezes)* I'm sorry – It's nice to meet you but –

(sneezes)

What the hell, Pete?

THOMAS. Oh, no.

PETE. I thought it would be a nice surprise? Real tree, for a real Christmas?

JULIA. I'm allergic. You know that!

THOMAS. But I really love real Christmas trees, Jules. And we never got to have them as kids. Because of you.

JULIA. It's not like I was allergic ON PURPOSE, Peter!

EMILY. You know what? I should head home. It was really nice meeting you all –

ALISON. Hope to see you soon, Emily!

*(**CHARLIE** comes careening down the stairs in his karate outfit.)*

CHARLIE. Bye, Emily! This is my karate outfit!

EMILY. Lookin good!

*(to **PETE**)*

It was nice meeting you.

PETE. You too.

(**EMILY** *exits. A beat.* **JULIA** *sneezes.*)

ALISON. Peter, you need to ask that girl out on a date.

JD. Yeah, she's awesome.

CHARLIE. She likes you.

PETE. What? No. I'm still a married man.

ALISON. You're one signed form away from being single –

JULIA. And one REAL Christmas tree away from being homeless.

THOMAS. I have a plan! First, EVERYONE STOP EATING MY LEFTOVERS.

    (**JD** *and* **ALISON** *put down their food.*)

    Thank you. Second – men – at attention! We will have our REAL Christmas tree –

JULIA. We will?

THOMAS. Yes! Right outside the kitchen window. And we can decorate BOTH trees.

    (*mostly to himself*)

    Two Christmas trees. It sounds like a new tradition to me. I love this.

PETE. Ok! That sounds great. I'm sorry, Jules –

JULIA. *(sneezing)* It's fine. Just get this thing out of here, okay?

THOMAS. C'mon, men!

    (**CHARLIE**, **TOM**, **JD** *and* **PETE** *grab the Christmas tree – stand and all – and haul it outside.*)

    (*We see them outside of the Kitchen window fussing with it to get it to stand up straight.*)

    (**JULIA** *sinks down on the couch.* **ALISON** *approaches.*)

JULIA. My house is a mess. I have a grown, lonely man living on my couch. I haven't even started my shopping yet. What have I done?

ALISON. You are being an amazing sister. And suffering the consequences. But Pete needs this. You were right. He needs to be near his friends.

JULIA. So would you and JD take him in?

ALISON. God no.

JULIA. Alison –

ALISON. You are the compassionate one. I'm the bitchy one. It's our thing. I think that Pete's just afraid of starting over. He hates change – but all he needs is a nudge in the right direction.

JULIA. I know you're right. But I have a strong urge to just kick in the pants instead –

ALISON. I think I've got an idea. To help Pete realize that it's time to move on with his life. That he doesn't need Margaret after all. What are your plans for Christmas Eve?

JULIA. Whatever you've got cooking up.

ALISON. We're having a party. And we're going to invite Emily…

(CRASH!)

*(**JULIA** and **ALISON** jump and turn around. The boys have managed to push the Douglas Fir through the kitchen window. The top of the tree hangs in over the kitchen counter.)*

PETE. *(OS)* Oops! Sorry!

CHARLIE. *(OS)* TIMBER!!!

*(**JULIA** looks like she's about to run out the door and murder everyone. She starts for the exit, but **ALISON** grabs her and pulls her into a bear hug. She begins singing a song in the style of "It's the most wonderful time of the year."*)*

(Fade to black.)

---

*The publisher recommends that the licensee creates an original composition that stays true to the authors' intent.

ACT TWO

Scene One

(A Montage, which will be underscored by a song in the style of "It's the Most Wonderful Time of the Year" about how great the holiday season is and how much everyone loves it and how EVERYONE IS VERY HAPPY AND NOT GOING TOTALLY CRAZY.)*

(We are watching time progress – one month, from Black Friday to Christmas Eve, should unfold in a succinct, quasi-ballet. Uh, but without dancing and stuff. Or they can dance, playing out the beats in time with the music. Whatever you want.)

(Over the course of this scene, Thanksgiving will disappear and Christmas will arrive in all of its cheerful glory.)

(NOTE: Whenever a character exits the stage, they should return in a new shirt or outfit, to help illustrate the passage of time (probably lots of sweaters). One production used T-shirts to illustrate the passing of days "21 days until Christmas," "14 days until Christmas," and so on.)

*(Whenever **PETE** exits the stage, regardless of what he is doing, he must also re-enter with an armful of dirty laundry, which he places in a pile DSC. This pile should be comically large by the end of the montage.)*

---

*The publisher recommends that the licensee creates an original composition that stays true to the authors' intent.

(Beats of the montage:)

*(***THOMAS*** *and* ***PETE*** *remove the tree from the window (from outside).* ***JULIA*** *sweeps the glass up in the kitchen.* ***JD*** *tapes a piece of cardboard over the broken window.* ***ALISON*** *and* ***CHARLIE*** *pick at the turkey carcass.* ***JULIA*** *whips out a black trash bag, grabs the turkey carcass from* ***ALISON*** *and* ***CHARLIE*** *and stuffs it in the trash. All characters on stage (***CHARLIE, JULIA, JD, ALISON***) exit.)*

*(***THOMAS*** *and* ***PETE*** *enter the front door with a mostly-decorated tree. They set it up where the real tree was. They exit.)*

*(***JULIA*** *enters (in a new outfit) and begins furiously scrubbing the kitchen counter.* ***PETE*** *enters (in a new outfit) and begins putting food on the counter where* ***JULIA*** *is cleaning.* ***JULIA*** *moves the food.* ***PETE*** *moves it back.* ***THOMAS*** *and* ***CHARLIE*** *enter (in new outfits) and sit down to play a video game.* ***PETE*** *is distracted from making his snack, leaves everything on the counter, and goes to join them.* ***JD*** *bursts through the door and joins them…with Doritos (which probably go everywhere).* ***JULIA*** *exits.* ***ALISON*** *enters with her briefcase, and claps her hands at the lazy men, who scatter and exit (all except* ***PETE***, *who she has a meeting with). They begin reviewing documents in her briefcase.* ***PETE*** *gets upset.* ***ALISON*** *exits.* ***EMILY*** *enters through the front door with a lovely Poinsettia plant and places it on the kitchen counter. She scurries to the couch, and upset* ***PETE*** *turns into genuinely happy* ***PETE***. *He sprints offstage.)*

*(***JULIA*** *enters the front door with SO MANY BAGS of groceries.* ***EMILY*** *goes to help her bring everything inside.* ***JULIA***, *happy and exhausted, gives* ***EMILY*** *a hug.)*

*(***EMILY*** *goes to leave, but is stopped by* ***ALISON*** *who bursts through the door and swoops her back into the kitchen.* ***ALISON*** *pulls a bottle of wine out of her purse and pours glasses for* ***EMILY*** *and* ***JULIA***. *They*

drink (wine for **EMILY** *and* **JULIA,** *a gallon of milk for* **ALISON***) and have a "business meeting." ***ALISON*** exits into the bathroom. ***THOMAS*** opens the front door, finishes hanging a wreath outside, and steps in. As he enters,* **EMILY** *exits and they greet each other warmly.)*

*(***PETE*** enters and sits on the couch. He carries a box of tissues and turns on a movie on the TV (we don't hear or see it, but it's totally Sleepless in Seattle). He watches the movie and cries.* **JD** *walks over and tries to make him feel better. It doesn't work.* **JD** *hands him a box of tissues and exits.* **CHARLIE** *runs in with another tissue box and hands it to* **PETE***. He runs off.* **THOMAS** *and* **ALISON** *enter together, both with tissue boxes. They both try to talk to* **PETE***, but he's too busy watching his movie and crying. They hand him the tissue boxes and leave.)*

*(***ALISON*** enters and begins hanging Christmas lights/ garlands around the stage.* **PETE** *gets up from the couch and tries to help. He gets tangled in the lights. More crying.)*

*(***JD*** enters with a huge tray of cookies.* **CHARLIE** *and* **THOMAS** *run on stage. The boys descend on the tray, but* **ALISON** *enters from the front door, picks up the cookies and exits out the front door with them. The boys run after her.* **JULIA** *exits upstairs.)*

*(***EMILY*** and* **PETE** *enter.* **EMILY** *is carrying Mistletoe and* **PETE** *has a ladder.* **PETE** *climbs up the ladder.* **EMILY** *holds it steady for him.* **EMILY** *hands him the mistletoe and he hangs it up, then climbs down. They are now standing underneath the mistletoe, which they both realize at the same time.* **PETE** *gets suddenly bashful. He checks his watch. Gestures to the door. She nods and exits. He exits.)*

*(***JULIA*** enters, wobbling down the stairs with a massive stack of presents, which cover her face. She enters the living and trips over* **PETE***'s HUGE pile of laundry. A silent scream.* **PETE** *comes scurrying into the room, like*

*a dog with his tail between his legs. **JULIA** gestures to the laundry. CLEAN IT UP her body language yells. She storms offstage. **PETE** looks around, picks up his laundry and carries it over to the closet. He stuffs it inside. This may take several trips. It should be hard to fit all the laundry in there – but somehow, he manages it. He shuts the door, pleased with this genius, and plops down on the couch.)*

(The lights fade all the way up, and the scene begins.)

(Christmas Eve.)

*(**PETE** sits on the couch in pajama pants. **JULIA** re-enters with another stack of presents. She walks over to the tree and begins placing them underneath it.)*

PETE. I cleaned up my laundry!

JULIA. It's a Christmas miracle. Thank you.

(a beat)

Could you bring over those presents I dropped?

PETE. Sure!

*(**PETE** grabs a few of the gifts and brings them to **JULIA**.)*

Are you mad at me?

JULIA. People will be here any minute. Maybe put some pants on?

PETE. Cause you seem a little grumpy.

JULIA. Seriously, Pete? Put a real pair of pants on. JD and Alison will be here soon.

PETE. I don't really feel like going to this party, Jules. I'm emotionally exhausted. I just want to sit in my PJs and be comfy while my heart continues to break, okay? I'll be on the bottom bunk if anyone needs me.

JULIA. No, Pete. C'mon. This will be good for you. Everyone wants to see you – and it's Christmas Eve. You can't hide in Charlie's room alone.

PETE. Yes I can. I should get used to being alone, shouldn't I? I'm going to be alone for the rest of my life. At least I have *Sleepless in Seattle* to keep me company.

JULIA. Pete, you remember when we went to Niagara Falls when we were little? And you were scared of the water, so you cried for three days straight and kind of ruined the trip for everybody?

PETE. Yeah, I still have the keychain.

JULIA. THIS IS NIAGARA FALLS ALL OVER AGAIN. You are turning the holiday season into our family vacation from Hell. My living room has been your trash pile for the past month. You put a Douglas Fir through my kitchen window. You have single handedly made the A&P run out of Kleenex. Twice. And Pete, so help me, you better be using those tissues for <u>tears</u>. I love you, I want you to feel better. I've watched *Sleepless in Seattle* with you five times so far. The least you can do for me is put on a pair of pants and drink a scotch with your friends. For god's sake we have shrimp.

PETE. I love shrimp.

JULIA. I know you love shrimp! I got them for you. Because I love you, dummy.

(A beat.)

PETE. Thank you. And I will fix that window, Jules. I promise.

JULIA. I know you will. Now please. Pants.

PETE. Okay.

*(**PETE** sprints up the stairs to change.)*

*(**JULIA** goes into the kitchen to check on the dinner in the oven. She pauses at the sink, reaches in, and pulls out a sock.)*

JULIA. You have got to be kidding me.

*(A knock at the front door, then **ALISON** and **JD** enter. **JD** is carrying a MASSIVE flower arrangement. **ALISON** looks like she is going to have her baby right now.)*

ALISON. I swear to God, Julia, you are the only person I will put real clothes on for.

JD. It's true. She's spent the last three weeks wearing a muumuu. The same muumuu. Which is a thing they still make, surprisingly.

JULIA. Thank you, Ali. At least someone is willing to wear clothes on Christmas Eve. The flowers are beautiful. Thanks, JD.

JD. Well last time I was here it stank like socks. So, I figured this might help.

(**JULIA** *hands him the sock she pulled from the sink.*)

This better be yours.

JULIA. It is not.

JD. Gross! Oooh, shrimp!

(**JD** *wanders to the shrimp on the counter.*)

ALISON. *(to* **JULIA***)* How are you holding up?

JULIA. I almost broke my neck tripping over a pile of clothes the size of a small horse this morning, but other than that, I'm great.

(**ALISON** *makes a gesture to* **JD** *to leave the ladies alone.* **JD** *notices and nods.*)

JD. *(mouth full)* Where're Thomas'n'Pete?

JULIA. Upstairs getting ready.

JD. *(stiff, to* **ALISON** *as if to a Captain)* Then that is where I will go, too.

(not stiff)

Man time!

(He runs upstairs to join his friends.)

ALISON. Julia. This is your busy season. You've been working double shifts at the restaurant, and last weekend you catered five different Holiday parties.

JULIA. It's Christmas time – the People demand ham.

ALISON. I'm worried about you.

JULIA. Wow. Your mommy hormones have kicked into overdrive, huh?

ALISON. It's terrifying. I care about everyone now. I was watching TV yesterday, and a coffee commercial came on and I started crying.

JULIA. Oh! Was it the one with the little boy and his big brother is in the army and –

ALISON. I don't wanna talk about it.

JULIA. Well, I appreciate your concern. I'm just stretched a little thin.

ALISON. Ya think? If my brother came and made a garbage dump of my living room—no offense—I'd have him arrested and picking up cans on the highway before New Years. But that's just me. But you, Julia dear, are an extremely compassionate and understanding sister, and have earned yourself no fewer than four wines this evening. And the party will be great. It's Christmas Eve. You're cooking for your closest friends and family. And it's the first time we've had a guest since Pete got married to she-who-will-not-be-named.

JULIA. So – about the guest –

ALISON. You invited Emily, didn't you? Operation End the Wallow depends on –

JULIA. No, she's invited. I just – I didn't mention anything to Pete. Yet.

ALISON. Yet? She'll be here any minute. When were you planning on telling him?

JULIA. When she got here?

ALISON. We can't spring this on him! He'll think we're trying to set him up!

JULIA. We are trying to set him up.

ALISON. No we aren't. We are trying to help him see that he wasn't defined by his marriage. That there are other fish in the sea! Other cats in the kennel! Other –

JULIA. I barely got him to put pants on, Alison. We didn't have time to talk about fish or cats.

ALISON. I still don't understand why this tactic is better than just telling him she's coming.

JULIA. I didn't want him to flip out. Christmas Eve is a time for close family and friends. If I told him I invited Emily, he would know we were up to something, and he would have stapled his gross pajama pants to his body and locked himself in Charlie's toy trunk to avoid socializing. I was hoping that if his new lady friend Emily seemingly happened to show up, he might have the presence of mind to just enjoy her company. And be charming. And maybe not cry.

ALISON. So is that an argument for or against spiking his eggnog?

JULIA. Oh, we definitely need to get him drunk. And me drunk. What was that about four wines?

ALISON. On it. Just being around the liquor makes me feel better.

JULIA. Vicarious drinking?

ALISON. *(hands her a wine)* Something like that.

JULIA. I know Pete is still hurting from this divorce, but it's just been going on for so long now. I want to see Pete happy again. The new year is almost here, he just signed his divorce papers… This could be the fresh start that he needs. I think he might be finally ready to move on – or at least, you know, get out of my house.

ALISON. Listen, I was hoping this would get sorted out before Christmas…but Pete might not be as ready to move on as you think. Margaret's lawyers have been calling me non-stop. Pete still hasn't signed the divorce papers.

JULIA. He told me he signed those weeks ago.

ALISON. Yeah. And how's that window of your doing? Still broken?

JULIA. You've got to be kidding me.

ALISON. I'm not. But if anyone asks, it was my baby hormones that made me break attorney-client privilege and blab to you. Now excuse me. I have to take a tinkle.

(**ALISON** *exits.* **JULIA** *stews in the kitchen.*)

(**THOMAS**, **PETE**, **JD** *and* **CHARLIE** *come down the stairs.* **JD** *is holding the shrimp platter, which has been entirely consumed.*)

JD. Your brother sure knows how to destroy a shrimp cocktail, Jules.

CHARLIE. I had two shrimps and Uncle Pete had two hundred.

THOMAS. What? When was there shrimp?

JD. When you were Google-ing "How to tie a bowtie."

THOMAS. Julia! Those internet trolls ate all the shrimp!

PETE. Just 'cause Charlie is short doesn't mean you have to go calling him a troll, Thomas. That's a little harsh.

THOMAS. I was talking about you.

JD. Dude, only a programmer would use Trolls as an insult in real life.

(*JULIA opens the fridge and pulls out another shrimp platter. She puts it on the counter in front of* **THOMAS**.)

THOMAS. I MARRIED A GENIUS!

PETE. Ooh! More shrimp!

(**PETE** *goes to get another shrimp.* **JULIA** *slaps his hand away. Hard.*)

OW. WHY?

JULIA. You don't get more shrimp.

PETE. But I want to eat them.

JULIA. This platter of shrimp is for the boys and girls who are on Santa's "Nice" list.

CHARLIE. THAT's ME!

(**CHARLIE** *grabs a handful of shrimp*)

JULIA. Exactly. It's for good little boys like Charlie who do their chores and are nice to their parents and who don't tell lies – (*whisper-shouts in his ear*) – and who have signed their divorce papers!

PETE. I – No, I have no idea what you're talking about.

(*whisper shouting to* **JULIA**)

WHO TOLD YOU?

JULIA. Pete, will you help me put the crackers on a plate?

(*whisper shouting as they prep food*)

It doesn't matter who told me. You lied to me.

PETE. Triscuits or Wheat Thins?

(whisper shouting)

I did not!

JULIA. Half and half.

(Whisper shouting)

Yes you did. You said you signed those papers!

PETE. Is this Christmas Tree platter good for the snacks?

JULIA. No! The tree plate is for the Ham. Elves are for the snacks.

PETE. Julia, these are the exact same plate. Are you serious?

JULIA. ELVES are for SNACKS.

(whisper shouting)

And don't try to change the subject.

PETE. *(whisper shouting)* I said I was going to sign them! And I am! I mean, I will! I've just – I've been busy.

JULIA. *(shouting)* BUSY? YOU have been busy?

(**JD**, **THOMAS** *and* **CHARLIE** *look up from the shrimp platter and over at* **JULIA** *and* **PETE** *simultaneously.*)

PETE. *(to* **JD**, **PETE** *and* **TOM***)* Busy plating hors d'oeuvres.

JULIA. Hardly. Pigs in a blanket. Oven. Now. Please. Actually, I'll just handle it.

PETE. I'll get them.

JULIA. I don't think I can trust you not to drop them. Or to even remember that they are in an oven, baking, which is a time-sensitive process. One that requires attention, and timeliness. And SELF RESPECT. Get the mustard.

PETE. I HAVE SELF RESPECT. Here is your mustard. Can you please stop yelling at me? I'm not even sure what I did.

JULIA. Nothing, Pete! You did nothing. That's the point. You've completely stalled your life and you're missing all these opportunities to move on – to move forward.

PETE. That's not true! I want to move forward!

(**EMILY** *enters through the front door carrying a tray of cookies*)

EMILY. Hey everyone!

THOMAS/JD/CHARLIE. Hey!

PETE. (*Stares at* **EMILY**. *Then to* **JULIA**. *Then to* **EMILY**.) I'm going to go to Charlie's bunk bed now. Goodbye everyone.

(**PETE** *begins backing away from* **EMILY** *toward the stairs*)

Julia grabs Pete's arm before he can leave.

JULIA. Forward, Peter. Move forward.

CHARLIE. Hiya, Emily! I'll put those cookies on an elf platter for you. My mom is very particular about elves and snacks.

EMILY. Thanks, Charles!

ALISON. (*enters from the bathroom*) Hey. Jules. You're out of wrapping paper in there.

JULIA. I'll get some. Pete, why don't you offer Emily a drink?

(**JULIA** *glares at* **PETE** *and then exits upstairs.*)

PETE. Emily. I did not know you would be joining us at this family gathering. Of family. What are you doing here?

EMILY. Merry Christmas?

EVERYONE BUT PETE. Merry Christmas!

ALISON. I'll get you that drink. Pete, you should have a drink too. What can I get you two? Wine? Whiskey? Vodka? Valium?

JD. Viagra?

CHARLIE. What's that?

THOMAS. Medicine uncle JD needs. HEY-O! High five!

(**THOMAS** *high fives* **CHARLIE**, *who does not understand*)

EMILY. Wine for me, please.

(**JULIA** *enters with a few rolls of toilet paper.*)

JULIA. How are we all doing down here?

PETE. Julia, let me help you with all of that toilet paper.

JULIA. I got it –

> (**PETE** *grabs the rolls from her and pulls her off to the side of the bathroom door*)

Okay then –

PETE. *(whisper shouting)* Why is Emily here?

JULIA. *(whispering)* Do not be rude right now, Pete. I invited her over.

PETE. *(whisper shouting)* This is supposed to be a night for close friends and family. Last year I was here with my wife. This feels weird. I feel weird! I don't like this feeling! It's – I'm hot. It's hot. Is it hot? Are your hands sweaty? My hands are so sweaty. Feel them.

> (**PETE** *touches* **JULIA***'s face. She pulls back, horrified.*)

JULIA. Pete. Pull it together.

> (**ALISON** *hands wine to* **EMILY**. **THOMAS** *takes the whiskey and brings it over to* **PETE** *and* **JULIA**.*)

THOMAS. *(handing whiskey to* **PETE***, whispering)* What is going on over here?

PETE. My hands are dripping. Like two faucets. Feel.

> (**THOMAS** *grabs both of his wrists before* **PETE** *can touch his face.*)

JULIA. Mild panic attack. He'll be fine.

PETE. *(loudly)* No, I won't be fine! I'm going to be alone for the rest of my life!

CHARLIE. Hey Uncle Pete? You're not alone right now. Why don't you come have some grape juice with me?

> (**PETE** *looks at* **CHARLIE** *for a long moment and nods. He takes a few calming breaths and walks over to the living room couch.*)
>
> (*He sits on the floor next to his nephew and drinks* **CHARLIE***'s grape juice.*)

EMILY. Do you want a cookie or something, Pete?

PETE. Is there any more shrimp left?

JD. Sure thing, buddy.

(**JD** *passes the shrimp plate over.* **PETE** *grabs a few shrimp.*)

PETE. I'm sorry I kind of yelled over there. I don't know what came over me.

EMILY. Believe me, I get it. You should have seen me two Christmases ago. After my husband passed. My parents came over for the Holidays and we went to the tree lighting in town. There was this young couple in front of us, just all over each other – making out, all touchy feely – in public. Total PDA. And I lost it. I started shouting at them about boundaries and conduct unbecoming the youth of America and Christmas spirit and the baby Jesus. I made them cry. And that was before I found the mulled cider tent. It went downhill from there. I've been banned from the town tree lighting ceremonies for the next three years.

THOMAS. The holidays do crazy things to everyone. In a relationship, out of a relationship… Remember that time I crashed your family Christmas dinner? It was before Julia and I "officially" started dating. We were both back home from college on winter break – I had asked her to go ice skating with me on Christmas Eve and she said no – something about grocery shopping and ham and adult responsibility – and I was totally heartbroken. And a little crazed, so I called your mom and told her this story about how my parents left town without me, because they forgot I was coming home –

JD. Isn't that the plot of Home Alone?

THOMAS. Yup. Pretty much. I left out the bit about burglars. And also I was 20 years old and not 8. But the sympathy card totally worked and your mom insisted I come join your family for dinner and STAY THE NIGHT. I was in heaven. I slept on the floor of the hallway outside of Julia's room that night, just to be close to her –

ALISON. Creepy.

JULIA. I thought it was sweet.

ALISON. It was creepy.

THOMAS. I was in love. What do you want from me?

PETE. Dad wanted you to get the hell out of our house.

THOMAS. Ah, he warmed up to me. Eventually. Right?

(**JULIA** *and* **PETE** *exchange a look.*)

JULIA/PETE. Yeah! Sure! Totally! He kind of loves you!

JD. Well… That sounds like a "no" to me.

(**ALISON** *slaps the back of* **JD** *'s head.*)

ALISON. Do not give him a hard time about reciprocated parent-in-law love.

JD. Why? Your parents love me.

(**ALISON** *gives him a look.*)

JULIA. Yeah, JD, but Alison had a slightly harder time if you'll recall.

JD. What are you talking about? My parents love you, Alison! My mom can't stop asking me about how you're doing every time she calls.

ALISON. *(grabs a bowl of potato chips and begins snacking)* She's not asking about me. She's asking about this alien growing inside of me.

CHARLIE. *(Totally terrified)* What alien?

PETE. Aunt Alison is hyperbolizing, Charlie.

CHARLIE. What does that even mean?

JD. It means she's full of –

JULIA. She has a baby growing inside her. Not an alien.

(**CHARLIE** *moves further away from* **ALISON** *just to be on the safe side.*)

ALISON. All I'm trying to say is that I understand Tom's pain. I wasn't exactly your mom's favorite person when we started dating – or since. I mean, you ruin one little Easter Dinner and it's like you're marked for life.

EMILY. This sounds epic.

JD. Oh. It was.

ALISON. I don't want to talk about it.

THOMAS. Too bad. We do.

JD. It was the first time Alison ever came over for a family dinner, and –

ALISON. You aren't setting this up right.

JD. You said you didn't want to tell the story. So I'M gonna tell the story. Okay?

ALISON. Fine.

JD. So Alison comes over and my ma and my aunts are the most excited I've ever seen –

ALISON. His six aunts. Six.

JD. My Mom comes from a huge family, and Easter is a big Holiday in our house so –

ALISON. Everyone was there. Must have been like, 45 people packed into this two-bedroom ranch house.

(*JD gives* **ALISON** *a look and clears his throat.*)

JD. And Alison was going to be the main attraction. They couldn't wait to meet her. And my ma and my aunts couldn't wait to get her into the kitchen and cook with her.

JULIA. Oh god. No.

THOMAS. Why would anyone ever want Alison in the kitchen?

ALISON. HEY! My Mashed potatoes this year were a huge success.

CHARLIE. All that garlic made my tummy hurt.

ALISON. Shut up, kid.

JD. Well, you see, I mighta been exaggerating a little about the prowess of my woman in the kitchen.

ALISON. Your woman?

JD. My – ah. My lady friend?

ALISON. Try again.

JD. My love.

EMIL. So you basically lied to your family and said Alison was a good cook?

JD. Well, I mean, lie is such a harsh –

ALISON. Yes. That's exactly what happened.

JD. Do you want to tell this story or what?

ALISON. Let's just wrap this up, shall we? Basically they wanted me to Osso Busco some lamb and I ended up setting the stove on fire. And one of JD's Aunts – Aunt… oh hell, I can never remember all their names.

JD. AUNT AGATA. For chrissakes you'd think you'd be able to remember the woman you lit on fire!

ALISON. They all have crazy names! And who goes near a stove that's on fire? That is on her. No sane jury would convict me.

EMILY. Oh my god. Was she okay?

ALISON. Oh, she was fine. Singed her moustache a little – which in my opinion helped her in the long run. No permanent damage, though.

JD. Except for my ma's kitchen.

ALISON. Oh, right.

JD. And the entire meal.

EMILY. What did you do?

ALISON. JD and I introduced them to a family tradition of mine – we all went to Ruby Tuesday's. And you know something? His mom has served Onion Straws at every Easter since, so I personally think it was a huge success.

EMILY. *(a toast)* Here's to Holidays that are huge successes, even when they are total disasters.

(Everyone cheers to this except for **PETE**. *He sits on the couch, shaking his head.)*

PETE. Those are all good stories, you guys, but they don't make me feel any better. You're all talking about the people that you love – but I don't have that. Nobody loves me enough to marry me even after I burn their mom's house down. Nobody would sleep on the floor outside of my bedroom or yell at handsy teenagers because they miss me. I don't have any of that. I thought I did. For five years I thought I had that. But I don't. I never had that. I don't have anybody that loves me like that because I don't have a family.

(JULIA *looks stricken.* TOM, ALISON, EMILY *and* JD *exchange a quick glance.*)

EMILY. Pete, c'mon.

PETE. No. It's the truth. I don't have a family to love or take care of anymore. I'm alone.

THOMAS. Are you serious?

JD. Dude. You're in a room full of people who care about you. You're, like, the least alone person there is. We're your family.

PETE. Oh really? Are you going to go antique shopping with me and pick out a coffee table that matches the new couch? Are you going to help me shave my back when I need to be manscaped? Are you going to be my little spoon in the middle of the night?

JD. No way dude.

ALISON. And I doubt Margaret did any of those things, either.

PETE. She – THAT's NOT THE POINT!

THOMAS. Hey, Charlie? Why don't you show Emily your ninja warrior army? She hasn't seen it yet.

CHARLIE. Oh cool! C'mon Emily!

(EMILY *glances at the other adults and follows* CHARLIE *upstairs.*)

PETE. I'm just being honest. Your little love stories aren't going to help me. I'm trying to tell you how I feel.

(THOMAS *is ready to unleash on* PETE *– but before he can get a word out—*)

JULIA. How you FEEL? That's all you've been doing for the past four weeks. We are DEEPLY aware of how you feel, Peter and we have all been working our butts off to try to find a way to make you comfortable and happy which, apparently, is impossible.

PETE. I'm heartbroken, Julia! What do you want from me?

JULIA. I want you to act like a person! Look around you! Look at these people. We love you. Even Emily thinks you're nice which absolutely blows my mind since you've been doing a really convincing impersonation of a wet mop the entire time she's known you.

PETE. Oh! I'm sorry! I'm sorry I'm not acting the way you want! My marriage is crumbling around me, but here – let me put on my happy face for my big sister so she won't get mad at me.

(**PETE** *makes an absurd happy face.*)

JULIA. Well it's better than how you look usually! Like a dumb sad clown!

(**JULIA** *makes a dumb sad clown face. They continue to make faces at each other.*)

PETE. Stop it!

JULIA. You stop it first!

(Neither one stops it.)

PETE. What, you don't like my manic happy face? This is how you look all the time! "Oh! I'm so important with my successful restaurant and my perfect family! I'm stressed out but I can't let anyone see that ever because then I won't be perfect!"

JULIA. "Oh boo-hoo. My marriage that I didn't even like that much is finally over and I'm just going to give up everything I love, except for Sleepless in Seattle, and wallow for the rest of my life."

PETE. *(stops making his face)* That's not funny, Julia! That's mean!

ALISON. Can you guys just stop? I want to take both of you over my knee and spank you right now.

JD. That's hot.

ALISON/THOMAS/PETE/JULIA. Shut up, JD!

JD. No, YOU GUYS shut up! Man…

JULIA. You and Margaret have been separated for over a year, Pete. This divorce sucks, but it's not a shock. It's been a long time coming – and yet you REFUSE to move on. You can't sign those divorce papers even though you know you will be better off once it's officially over. You're so afraid of being alone you don't realize that you aren't. You have a family.

PETE. Oh yeah? Who's my family?

ALL. Us!

JD. Ya dummy.

PETE. Some family. Two friends who will always be closer with their wives than me, a lawyer who only likes me because I own an in-ground pool, and a sister who won't even support me while I go through the hardest time in my life. I don't belong here. You don't want to help me – all you want to do is push me to "let go" and "feel better" and get back to "normal."

(**EMILY** *enters from upstairs.*)

THOMAS. Julie is trying to help you, Pete. We all are. We love you and we want to see you happy.

PETE. (*re:* **EMILY**) Oh sure. Is that why you brought Emily here? To show me that there are other fish in the sea –

(*to* **EMILY**)

You are much prettier than a fish, and you are much lovelier and friendlier than a fish, too. It's just a metaphor.

(*to* **JULIA**)

The only fish I'm interested in right now is shrimp.

JD. Is there still shrimp left?

THOMAS. Pete, don't you think it's time to start moving on?

PETE. Yeah, you're right. I'll move on. I'm outta here. I don't need to be around all of you perfect people with your perfect lives and your perfect families reminding me how much of a mess I am. Trying to fix me. Telling me how to deal with MY divorce. How to manage MY wardrobe. I'm a successful dentist and I know how to take care of myself. I just have to grab a few things and I'll be out of your hair. FOREVER.

(**PETE** *storms over to the closet and yanks open the door. ALL OF THE CLOTHES EVER tumble out at* **PETE.** **PETE***'s "dignified" exit has turned into a total disaster. He hastily grabs a few random articles of clothing and a big box filled with wrapped presents that was also in the closet.*)

(re: the presents)

I'm taking these with me. They were for my friends, but you can't have them anymore. Because you're mean.

JD. C'mon, dude. You don't have to be like that.

(**PETE** *throws open the front door, then marches back into the living room and with his free hand grabs the shrimp platter. He storms back to the door.*)

PETE. Merry Christmas and goodbye FOREVER.

(**PETE** *tries to slam the door behind him but his arms are full, so it's awkward. Everyone just watches him. He eventually manages to close the door (or not, and bails, whatever works.)*)

(A beat.)

(**THOMAS** *hugs* **JULIA.** **EMILY** *and* **ALISON** *look concerned. Then:*)

JD. I can't believe he took the shrimp.

(Lights Fade, Transition To:)

Scene Two

(Another montage, underscored by a song in the style of "Blue Christmas" or another equally depressing (yet somehow up-tempo) Christmas melody.)*

(Beats of the montage that illustrate the passage of time from Christmas Eve to New Year's Eve:)

*(**THOMAS** brings out a laundry hamper and exits. **JD**, **ALISON** and **EMILY** shovel **PETE**'s dirty laundry into the hamper before exiting. **JULIA** is left on stage alone.)*

*(**THOMAS** appears in pajamas, holding a robe and a cup of coffee. He puts the robe on **JULIA** and hands her the mug. He moves the laundry hamper into the bathroom and joins **JULIA** on the couch. **CHARLIE** runs down the stairs like a maniac.)*

*(**CHARLIE** opens a present on the living room floor as **JULIA** watches on somberly. **THOMAS** comforts her.)*

*(**CHARLIE** grabs an armful of wrapped presents from under the tree and runs upstairs with them.)*

*(**JULIA** removes her robe, hands it to **THOMAS**. **THOMAS** grabs an armful of presents and walks offstage with them.)*

*(Only a handful of gifts are left under the tree. **JULIA** looks at them sadly. They were **PETE**'s presents.)*

*(**JULIA** dumps her coffee in the sink, retrieves a bottle of wine from the counter, and opens a cabinet to get a glass – but instead she discovers one of **PETE**'s shirts, which had been crammed in. She pulls it out, holds it up and starts crying. She runs offstage.)*

*(**JULIA** enters with a laundry hamper, dressed in a cocktail dress. She sits down on the couch and begins folding laundry.)*

---

*The publisher recommends that the licensee creates an original composition that stays true to the authors' intent.

(The montage is over and the lights fade up:)

(New Year's Eve.)

*(***JULIA*** *continues to fold laundry – it's all of* **PETE**'*s clothes. She pulls them out of a hamper and folds them next to her on the couch. It's a sad, methodical process. She clearly misses* **PETE**. *She checks her phone intermittently, hoping for a message from him.)*

(The pile of presents under the tree is gone. Now, only a few wrapped gifts remain – they are for **PETE**. *He never came over for Christmas.)*

*(***THOMAS*** *enters, looking quite dapper in a suit and tie.)*

THOMAS. *(modeling)* Near year, new suit! What do you think?

JULIA. *(glancing at her phone, not at her husband)* Looks nice, babe.

THOMAS. Jules, c'mon.

JULIA. I'm sorry. It's just – I called Pete like, fifteen times yesterday to tell him about the party at my restaurant. I was just hoping he would have gotten back to me now to tell me if he's going to come or not.

THOMAS. Julia, you have to stop worrying about him, okay? We all need some time away from each other right now.

JULIA. We haven't seen him since that fight on Christmas Eve and it's been almost a full week.

THOMAS. Pete is pouting. We can't keep –

(notices the laundry)

Are you – is that Pete's laundry?

JULIA. I had to keep my mind off of the fight. So I did a few loads.

THOMAS. *(holding up a pair of pants)* Did you iron these? You never iron my pants. You got the pleats in them and everything!

JULIA. Don't wrinkle them.

THOMAS. Why are you doing his laundry? In a party dress? Stop folding!

JULIA. I just – I feel bad, Tom. Okay?

THOMAS. Why? Pete's the one who stormed out. You didn't do anything wrong.

JULIA. Tom –

THOMAS. Listen to me. Pete has been coddled his entire life. You do it, your mother does it – even our eight year old son does it. It's one of the reasons I didn't want you to invite him to stay with us – he doesn't need to be taken care of anymore. He needs to start taking care of himself.

JULIA. But Pete was right. We all could have been more supportive. I never really took the time to comfort him. Not like I should have. I was too busy fussing about all the laundry all over the place and now – I miss it. I miss his laundry all over the living room floor.

THOMAS. Yeah?

JULIA. Yeah!

*(**THOMAS** grabs a handful of laundry from the hamper and throws it on the floor.)*

THOMAS. How does that look.

JULIA. *(laughing)* It looks like it's missing something.

*(**JULIA** throws a handful of laundry on the floor.)*

That feels good!

(She overturns the hamper of clean clothes, scattering laundry all over the living room.)

THOMAS. *(grabs a sock)* One finishing touch.

(he runs to the kitchen and puts the sock in the sink)

JULIA. *(her laughter turns into a sob)* All that's missing now is Pete.

THOMAS. Oh, Jules. C'mere.

*(**THOMAS** hugs **JULIA**.)*

JULIA. I just wanted to help him. He was sad. He's been sad for so long. I thought I was doing a good thing by pushing him to move on.

THOMAS. Well, you can be a bit pushy.

JULIA. Hey!

THOMAS. Kidding. It came from a sweet, genuine place, Jules. But Pete's a successful dentist. He'll find his own way. He just needs some time. Just watch, before you know it, he'll be bursting through that door with another garbage bag full of laundry.

(The front door bursts open. It's not **PETE***. It's* **ALISON** *and* **JD***. They are dressed up as well.* **ALISON** *makes a b-line for the bathroom.)*

JD. Happy New Year's Eve!

ALISON. Gotta pee!

*(***ALISON*** slams the bathroom door behind her.)*

JD. Whoa, what happened in here? Is Pete back!?

*(***JULIA*** cries even more.)*

I guess that answers that.

JULIA. Have you heard from him at all?

JD. No, Jules. He's been radio silent with us, too. Honestly, Pete kicking himself out was probably the best thing for everyone.

JULIA. You really think so?

JD. I don't know. Sure, I guess?

JULIA. *(hugs* **JD***)* Thank you.

THOMAS. Seriously? I've been saying that for a week and you just kept glaring at me! C'mon. Where's my hug?

ALISON. *(enters from the bathroom)* You know, you get to a certain point in your pregnancy where every time you go to the restroom you think, "What if the baby just slides out right now?"

JULIA. Trust me – you'll wish it were that easy when the time comes.

ALISON. I'm just saying, all that anxiety makes going to the bathroom really hard. And ugh! My body feels like it was run over by a semi truck. This kid needs to vacate the premises ASAP.

JD. Can we, like, not talk about this? It makes me uncomfortable.

JULIA. You're going to be a delight in the delivery room.

JD. Seriously you guys. My tummy starts jumping when we talk about this and I feel like I'm having one of Pete's panic attacks. My hands are all sweaty. Feel.

ALISON. Touch me with those sweaty hands and I will cut them off. I'm uncomfortable enough as it is.

(The front door opens. Everyone looks expectantly towards it, hoping it's **PETE**, *but it's not. It's* **EMILY**, *who is also dressed up.)*

EMILY. Hey everyone! Sorry if I'm –

(She notices the clothes on the floor) Oh my gosh! Is **PETE** *back?)*

JULIA. No.

THOMAS. Julia and I were feeling a little nostalgic is all.

JULIA. I think I've had my fill. Now I just want the mess cleaned up again.

*(***THOMAS** *and***JULIA** *begin picking up the clothes.)*

THOMAS. Listen, Emily, I'm so sorry about Christmas Eve –

EMILY. Tom, don't. You, Julia, JD and Alison have all apologized to me. It's not necessary. It was a family argument and it didn't even register on the Richter scale.

And besides, Pete said I was lovelier than a fish. So I've got that going for me. If you wanted to see what a REAL family fight looks like, you should've come over to my Mom's house on Christmas Day. My sister's boyfriend tried to lecture us all on the benefits of being a Vegan and after two hours, my Dad threatened him with the star ornament from the top of the Christmas tree.

*(***EMILY** *helps them pick up a few articles of clothing.* **JD** *joins in as well.)*

ALISON. It sounds entertaining.

EMILY. Yeah, for everyone except poor Franklin. The only thing we had in the house he could eat were clementines. It was tragic.

ALISON. Hand me some of those shirts – I'll fold 'em since I can't bend down to get them.

(The gang works together to pick up the mess. It's methodical and loving all at once.)

EMILY. I know I didn't exactly meet Pete when he was feeling his best – but your kid brother is a pretty good guy. He's got some stuff to work through, but he's got a good heart.

JULIA. Says the woman who had her tree stolen by him.

EMILY. I didn't say he wasn't weird.

THOMAS. We're just sorry you had to see us all like that. I'm sure Pete is too.

JD. I hope he is. He was acting like the animal the Virgin Mary rode to Bethlehem on if you catch my drift.

ALISON. A donkey?

JD. *(Crosses to* ALISON *and hands her some folded shirts)* Woman, why do you always insist on ruining my jokes?

ALISON. Why do you always tell stupid jokes?

*(*JD *kisses* ALISON *and sits next to her on the couch, rubbing her belly.)*

JD. You'll like my jokes, won't you, little man?

THOMAS. No way.

JD. Shut up, dude!

(Everyone laughs.)

*(*PETE *appears in the dining room window. He presses his hands and face against the glass. He sees everyone laughing and frowns. Maybe they didn't miss him after all?)*

*(*CHARLIE *bounds down the stairs wearing a suit, with his karate belt tied around the outside of his jacket.)*

CHARLIE. I'm ready for cake, the New Year AND any ninjas that are coming to the party. HIY – OH!

(Mid karate chop, **CHARLIE** *caught sight of* **PETE** *in the window)*

Uncle Pete!

JULIA. *(re: the laundry)* Oh, no, Charlie. I just got a little carried away doing the wash.

CHARLIE. No! Look!

*(***PETE** *ducks down. All the adults turn towards the window.)*

JULIA. Charlie, there's nobody there.

*(***CHARLIE** *marches over to the window and taps on the pane of glass.)*

CHARLIE. Uncle Pete! I know you're out there. And you probably feel really bad 'cause you and everyone were yelling the last time you were here. And 'cause you didn't get your Christmas presents. But we love you, okay?

THOMAS. Charlie – we all miss Uncle Pete, but –

*(***PETE** *slowly rises up, appearing inch by inch in the window a la the Elevator mime.)*

JD. Well look at that.

*(***CHARLIE** *marches over to the front door and opens it wide.)*

(A beat. **PETE** *disappears from the window.)*

(Another beat. Is he going to come inside?)

*(***PETE** *appears in the doorway, he has a messenger bag over his shoulder and he's holding an enormous pane of glass.)*

PETE. Hi.

JD. What the heck is that?

PETE. A peace offering.

(He walks over to **JULIA** *and* **THOMAS** *and hands them the pane of glass.)*

This is for the kitchen window that I broke. I called a window repair company and they're sending someone over on the 2nd to fix it.

THOMAS. You know those guys come with the glass right? You didn't have to –

JULIA. *(hands the glass to* **THOMAS***)* Tom. Shh.

(hugs **PETE***)*

Thank you.

PETE. I – uh. I wanted to apologize. To all of you.

JULIA. Pete, you don't have to –

THOMAS. No, he does. You were saying, Pete?

PETE. When I said I didn't have a family, I was being an idiot.

JD. Hear, hear!

ALISON. JD. Shh.

PETE. I don't think it's a big shock for anyone to hear me say that I don't really understand relationships. I didn't date very much in school, and nothing really made sense to me until Julia and Tom started seeing each other. And then they got married, and JD and Alison you guys got married and all of a sudden you guys had created these little families that were all your own. The two of you against the world. And I felt like I was being left behind – so when I met Margaret, I jumped into everything without thinking if she and I would make the *right* kind of family. We just…didn't fit the way you guys do. And it took me a really long time to realize that – I finally let myself believe it for the first time last week. Before Christmas, I thought maybe I wasn't ready to feel – happy again. So I fought against it. And it only took me one night alone at the Red Roof Inn for me to realize that you weird people are the most important humans in my life. And I came here because I needed to be around you and your craziness and to be here during the holidays because you are my family. And I am yours. And Emily, I know we haven't known each other that long, but I think you're the coolest person I've ever met, and I promise I'm not this strange all the time. And I got you this.

(**PETE** *pulls a pinecone out of his bag and hands it to* **EMILY**.)

So you can grow a new Douglas Fir in your front yard. And I promise I won't run this one over with my car, okay?

EMILY. *(laughing)* Okay. That sounds good.

JD. You know that won't be an actual tree for, like, 50 years, right? If it even grows at all…

EMILY. Well, we'll just have to plant it to find out, right Pete?

(**EMILY** *smiles at* **PETE**. *He grins back.*)

PETE. Charlie, this is for you –

CHARLIE. Wait, why are you giving us presents now Uncle Pete? It isn't Christmas anymore.

PETE. I know it's not Christmas day anymore – and I'm really sorry I missed that with you guys. I really am. But while I was sitting alone at the Red Roof Inn it donned on me that what Christmas is really about isn't what happens on December 25th – it's what we do the rest of the year – how we treat each other for those other 364 days –

CHARLIE. You mean what we do on all the days Santa's watching us?

PETE. Yeah. Just like that. And I was selfish this year. And these presents are a really small way for me to say I'm sorry I sucked for the last couple of months. And each present comes with the promise that I will be a better Uncle, brother and friend. Okay?

CHARLIE. Sounds like you're off to a good start, Uncle Pete. Santa's probably really impressed.

JULIA. We all are, Pete.

PETE. Awesome. So, Charlie, I got you these.

(He hands **CHARLIE** *nunchucks from his messenger bag.)*

CHARLIE. Whoa! Cool!

*(***THOMAS** *eases the nunchucks out of* **CHARLIE***'s hand.)*

THOMAS. Okay, sensei – I'll hang onto these until your karate teacher shows you how to use them without giving yourself a concussion.

PETE. And JD – this is for you –

(He pulls out a Jets onesie for an infant.)

JD. Oh man. Our baby can be a Jets fan from day 1, Ali.

ALISON. Good. It'll help him learn about disappointment from an early age.

PETE. And, Alison, these are yours.

(He hands her adult sized floaties.)

ALISON. Floaties?

PETE. You're not a very good swimmer, so you'll need them when you and the family come over to hang out in my pool.

ALISON. Your – wait. What?

EMILY. Pete, did you get your house back?

PETE. It took a few days to muster up my courage, but I called Margaret and we talked. It turns out, she's pretty miserable in a big house in the suburbs, and once I told her how much it meant to me, she gave it back. I'll help her with the brokers fee to find a new place for her in the city, but that's all she wants. She had her lawyers put everything in the divorce papers and –

ALISON. I really wish you would have talked to your own legal counsel first before –

JD. Alison. Shh.

JULIA. Pete, that's wonderful.

ALISON. About those papers. Have you –

PETE. This morning.

*(***PETE** *pulls the divorce papers out of his bag. They are in a manila envelope, stamped but not sealed.)*

I wanted you all to see them before I put it in the mail. Julia, you were right. I was afraid to sign the papers because I didn't want to end that chapter of my life – it felt too much like failure. But I've realized that these signed papers mark the start of the next chapter. Maybe I messed up the first time around, but it's almost a New Year, I've got the people I love most with me and I couldn't think of a better place for the next part of my life to begin.

(As **PETE** *talks, he should gesture with the papers. On the coffee table are several candles that are burning. Towards the end of his speech, in a grand gesture,* **PETE** *gestures the papers right into the flame of one of the candles. The divorce papers catch on fire.* **PETE** *doesn't notice until –)*

CHARLIE. Uncle Pete! The next chapter of your life is going up in flames!

PETE. What?

*(***PETE*** sees the papers are on fire)*

OH! Oh no!

*(***THOMAS*** grabs a dirty pot from the sink and runs it over to* **PETE**, *who drops the flaming papers inside.)*

It was signed by both of us… I had it notarized. WHY AM I BAD AT EVERYTHING?

ALISON. I'll get the latest version of the agreement from her lawyers and have a new copy for you in the morning, Pete.

THOMAS. See! It's no big deal! Besides, now your new chapter will officially start on the first day of the New Year.

JD. That's pretty poetic man.

PETE. You think?

EMILY. Totally. It was meant to happen this way.

JULIA. Absolutely.

(a beat)

I'm just gonna put these candles away though.

(*JULIA blows the candles out and carries them into the kitchen.*)

CHARLIE. Is it time to go to the party yet? And are you sure there's gonna be cake there?

THOMAS. Yes and yes, little man. You think your mom would throw a party without cake?

EMILY. You're coming to the party too, right Pete?

PETE. Yeah – I mean – if I'm still invited.

JULIA. Of course you are, little brother. I love you.

ALISON. (*struggling to get off the sofa*) Could someone just roll me out to the car?

EMILY. (*helps ALISON up*) When is the baby due, Alison?

ALISON/JD. Last week.

PETE. Maybe he's waiting to get his chapter started until the New Year, too.

ALISON. Maybe. All I know is that for every day he's late, I'm adding one more embarrassing photo to the album I'll eventually show his prom date.

(*JD opens the door for ALISON.*)

JD. I love you and you are beautiful.

ALISON. (*kisses JD*) You're not so bad yourself.

(*ALISON walks past JD. JD grins and swats her on the ass. The couple exits.*)

THOMAS. C'mon Charlie. Your cake awaits.

CHARLIE. WOO!

(*CHARLIE runs out the front door. THOMAS grabs JULIA's hand and pulls her in for a hug.*)

THOMAS. See? I told you everything would be okay.

JULIA. You are wise, sensei.

(*They kiss and exit.*)

(*EMILY and PETE remain on stage.*)

PETE. Emily, I – um. I just wanted to say that – I think you are – um. You know. And I – I would really like to – whoa.

Is it SUPER hot in here? Did someone just crank up the furnace or something? Because, I am the most overheated human being all of a sudden. Hah. Are you –

EMILY. You want to come over tomorrow for breakfast?

PETE. Yes.

EMILY. And maybe we can go to Home Depot and have someone show us how to plant a pine cone?

PETE. That sounds really nice.

(**EMILY** *takes* **PETE***'s hand and gives it a squeeze. She places her pine cone on the coffee table.*)

EMILY. *(re: the pine cone)* I'll come by and get it tomorrow.

PETE. I'll bring it over.

EMILY. Okay.

PETE. Okay.

EMILY. Happy New Year, Pete.

PETE. Yeah. Happy New Year.

(*They smile at each other and exit, still holding hands.*)

(*The lights fade, except for one that remains, just for a moment on the pine cone. Who knows if it'll ever grow into a majestic Douglas Fir, but hey, it's worth a try, right?*)

End of Play